Pat Hutchins

Greenwillow Books
An Imprint of HarperCollinsPublishers

Don't Forget the Bacon!
Copyright © 1976 by Pat Hutchins
All rights reserved. Manufactured in The United States of America.
For information address HarperCollins Children's
Books, a division of HarperCollins Publishers,
195 Broadway, New York, NY 10007.
www.harperchildrens.com

Library of Congress Cataloging-in-Publication Data
Hutchins, Pat
  Don't forget the bacon! / by Pat Hutchins.
    p.   cm.
  "Greenwillow Books."
  Summary: A little boy goes grocery shopping for his mother and tries hard to
remember her instructions.
  ISBN 0-688-80019-X — ISBN 0-688-84019-1 (lib. bdg.)
  ISBN 0-688-06787-5 (1987 Printing)
  ISBN 0-688-06788-3 (lib bdg. 1987 Printing) — ISBN 0-688-08743-4 (pbk.)
  [1. Stories in rhyme] I. Title.
PZ8.3.H965Do   75-17935
[E]   CIP
                                  AC

18 19 20 OPM 30 29 28 27 26 25 24

For Ben and Jeb Kidd

a cape for me?

41 The Cake Shop 41

41

fresh cream cakes